Keeping Secrets

As Elizabeth and Jessica approached Sweet Valley Middle School, a group of Jessica's Unicorn friends came over.

"There's something we want to discuss with you," Lila Fowler said. "Caroline told us you two have a secret language."

Jessica giggled nervously. "That girl is always saying all sorts of things."

"So she made it all up?" Lila asked suspiciously.

Jessica looked down at the ground. "No."

"Ha! She was right! How could you tell Caroline about this first? This is a huge insult to the Unicorns!"

"I didn't tell Caroline anything!" Jessica cried. "She just happened to overhear us speaking. . . ."

"Speaking what? Tell us, Jessica, tell us!"

All of the Unicorns were pressing in on Jessica. It was a difficult position to be in, and she didn't know how to get out of it. If she told them about Ithig, she'd be breaking the promise she'd made to her father and Elizabeth. But how could she keep a secret from the entire Unicorn Club?

Bantam Skylark Books in the SWEET VALLEY TWINS series
Ask your bookseller for the books you have missed.

#1 BEST FRIENDS
#2 TEACHER'S PET
#3 THE HAUNTED HOUSE
#4 CHOOSING SIDES
#5 SNEAKING OUT
#6 THE NEW GIRL
#7 THREE'S A CROWD
#8 FIRST PLACE
#9 AGAINST THE RULES
#10 ONE OF THE GANG
#11 BURIED TREASURE
#12 KEEPING SECRETS

SWEET VALLEY TWINS

Keeping Secrets

Written by
Jamie Suzanne

Created by
FRANCINE PASCAL

A BANTAM SKYLARK BOOK®
TORONTO · NEW YORK · LONDON · SYDNEY · AUCKLAND

RL 4, 008–012

KEEPING SECRETS
A Bantam Skylark Book / October 1987

*Produced by Cloverdale Press, Inc.
133 Fifth Avenue, New York, NY 10003*

Cover art by James Mathewuse

ISBN 0-553-15538-5

Published simultaneously in the United States and Canada

---

*Bantam Books are published by Bantam Books, Inc. Its trade-
mark, consisting of the words "Bantam Books" and the por-
trayal of a rooster, is Registered in U.S. Patent and Trademark
Office and in other countries. Marca Registrada. Bantam
Books, Inc., 666 Fifth Avenue, New York, New York 10103.*

PRINTED IN THE UNITED STATES OF AMERICA

O   0 9 8 7 6 5 4 3 2 1

To Jessica Ann Copskey

One

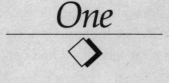

"I'm dying of curiosity!" Jessica Wakefield cried to her identical twin Elizabeth as they entered their house after school.

"Well, Dad should be home in about half an hour, and then we'll find out what this mystery is all about," said Elizabeth. She dropped her books on the counter of the Wakefields' Spanish-tiled kitchen and then poured herself a glass of milk.

"Did he give you any clue about what it is?" Jessica asked, her blue-green eyes sparkling.

Elizabeth sighed and threw up her hands. This was the third time that Jessica had asked her the same question. But Elizabeth could never stay annoyed at her sister for long. Being twins made them as close as any two people could be. From their long blond hair to the dimples in their left cheeks, they were exact doubles in appearance.

"All I know is that at breakfast this morning, after you left, Dad said he would tell us the secret tonight," Elizabeth said. "By the way, where did you go so early this morning?"

"I had Booster practice," Jessica told her. The Boosters were a cheering and baton squad that Jessica belonged to at school. "I just can't wait to hear this secret."

Elizabeth took her social studies book and sat down at the kitchen table. "Yes, I'm excited, too," she said, opening the book. "But right now I'm going to try to get some of my homework out of the way."

Her concentration was quickly broken by the sound of Jessica's fingernail tapping on the counter. Raising her head, she gave her sister a long, hard stare. "I'm trying to get some work done," she said.

But Jessica ignored her comment. She was much less concerned with things like homework than her hardworking twin. She never understood how Elizabeth could come home after a long day at school and start in immediately on her homework. "Maybe Dad's going to tell us that he's taking us on a trip to Europe!" Jessica declared. "Or maybe the secret is that we're finally getting a boat. . . ." She started to pace back and forth across the kitchen. "Maybe he's going to tell us that we have another twin—that we're really triplets!" she said, her blue-green eyes growing wide.

Elizabeth burst out laughing, remembering the time she and her sister pretended to have a triplet named Jennifer in order to pull a joke on their friend, Brooke Dennis. "I'm sure that would surprise Brooke!" she exclaimed, giggling. "Jessica, instead of letting your imagination run wild, why don't you try doing some of your homework?"

Jessica shook her head. "I'm too excited to sit still. I can't even think of doing homework right now!" She continued to pace across the room, her blond ponytail bouncing up and down with each step she took.

As she looked up at her sister, Elizabeth noticed the barrette that she'd just purchased. It was in Jessica's hair. "Hey, isn't that my barrette?" Elizabeth asked.

"Oh, this?" Jessica asked innocently, touching her hair with her fingers. Then, in her sweetest voice, she explained, "I noticed it sitting on your dresser for almost a week. I thought maybe you'd decided that you really didn't like it. . . ."

"You could have asked," Elizabeth said. Though she was used to Jessica borrowing her things without asking, it still bothered her.

"I promise I'll never borrow anything of yours again without asking first," Jessica assured her. "Here, you can have it back, big sister," she said, starting to remove the clip from her hair.

Elizabeth smiled. It was a running joke between the twins that Elizabeth was the "big sister" because she had been born four minutes earlier than Jessica. "That's all right, you can keep it. Besides, it looks better on you," Elizabeth said.

"How could it look better on me?" Jessica asked. "I mean, we look exactly the same."

"I'm not sure," Elizabeth admitted. "But if you say another word, I just might ask you to return it!"

Jessica smiled and clamped her hand over her mouth. "Don't worry, my lips are sealed!" she exclaimed.

I'll believe that when I see it, Elizabeth thought with a sigh.

Elizabeth started to read once again, and Jessica went over to the refrigerator and opened the door. "Look at this!" she exclaimed.

"What?" asked Elizabeth, closing her book. She wasn't going to get any work done with Jessica around.

"Look at all this food," said Jessica, opening the door wide enough for Elizabeth to see.

"I guess we beat Steven home," Elizabeth observed. Steven was the twins' older brother and a freshman at Sweet Valley High. Jessica and Elizabeth often joked that he could eat more than all of the Wakefields put together.

"Wow, this is great!" Jessica said as she removed a plate of brownies. "I'm glad we got here first!"

Jessica crammed a brownie into her mouth and was about to grab another one when Elizabeth warned her, "Don't spoil your appetite."

"Hmmm?" Jessica said.

"Dad's taking us out to eat because Mom's having dinner with a client," Elizabeth reminded her.

"Don't worry. I *never* lose my appetite," Jessica joked, reaching for yet another brownie. "Lizzie, what do you think the secret's going to be?"

Elizabeth shrugged.

"Don't you even have a guess?" Jessica asked.

Elizabeth had no idea about the secret, but just then another idea occurred to her. "Jess, why don't you and I make dinner for Dad? I think he'd really appreciate it. It'd be a real surprise and—"

"But we don't know how to cook," Jessica interrupted.

"That's not true. I can make spaghetti and you make a great salad."

Elizabeth could tell from the grimace on her sister's face that she wasn't exactly excited about the idea. "I want to go out," Jessica said firmly. "It'll be much more fun."

"OK, OK. It was only a suggestion," Elizabeth muttered.

When the twins had entered the sixth grade, Elizabeth noticed that their interests were beginning to take separate paths. Elizabeth liked to read and write and have long talks with her close friends. She was in charge of the *Sweet Valley Sixers*, the sixth-grade student newspaper at Sweet Valley Middle School. Jessica preferred cheering at basketball games and gossiping at meetings of the Unicorn Club, an exclusive all-girls club to which she belonged. She also loved to dance and took ballet lessons at Madam André's studio. But having different interests didn't stop them from being best friends. Though they'd grown in separate directions, Elizabeth felt there was no one in the world closer to her than Jessica, and she knew in her heart that Jessica felt the same way about her.

At that moment Elizabeth heard a loud noise and jumped up. At the same time Jessica gasped, her eyes growing wide and fearful. "W-what was that?" Jessica stammered in fright.

"I don't know," Elizabeth whispered, starting to tremble. Now she heard distinct footsteps coming up the basement steps. Someone was in the house! Was it a burglar? Elizabeth saw Jessica's tanned face instantly turn white as a sheet. She grabbed Jessica's arm tightly as the footsteps grew closer.

Then, to their horror, someone opened the basement door. They froze.

"What's going on? Are you two getting reacquainted?" Steven Wakefield asked as he walked in and saw his sisters with their arms around each other.

"Steven!" Elizabeth cried. "What are you doing here?"

"I live here, remember?" Steven replied.

"You mean you were home the whole time?" Elizabeth said, looking confused.

"We didn't think you were here. The refrigerator was full!" Jessica added. "You practically scared us to death!"

"I was downstairs doing my laundry," he reported matter-of-factly. Then he started dribbling an imaginary basketball. Aside from eating, basketball was Steven's favorite activity.

"You, doing laundry?" Elizabeth asked in disbelief.

"I didn't think you even knew how the washer worked," Jessica commented sarcastically.

"That's how much you know," Steven said, making a noise between a chuckle and a snort. Elizabeth thought Steven was the most immature fourteen-year-old she knew.

"I still don't understand why you were doing laundry," she continued.

"And I'd like to know why you didn't raid the refrigerator like you always do. Are you sick or something?" Jessica asked.

"Ha-ha. You guys think you're so smart. Since you're going out with Dad, I'm going out, too. I'm going to the Dairi Burger with some of the guys, and I wanted to save my appetite so I'd have room for at least two cheeseburgers, two chocolate shakes, and—"

"Stop!" Jessica cried as she bent over and clutched her stomach. "I'm getting sick just listening to this!"

"That still doesn't explain the laundry," Elizabeth observed.

"Can't a guy wear clean clothes? Mom's so busy these days that I have to do this myself. We all have to learn to help out." It was true that their mother, who had a job as a part-time interior designer, had been working long hours lately.

"Is this Steven Wakefield talking?" Jessica asked. "Mr. Big Deal High School Freshman? I remember when it was too much for you to carry a dish to the sink!"

Elizabeth was impressed. She'd never heard her brother sound this mature and responsible. He claimed that high school was changing him. Maybe, she silently admitted, he was right. The "old" Steven would never have given a moment's thought to helping out around the house.

"Now I've got to throw my stuff in the dryer," Steven announced, starting downstairs again. He turned around and added, "By the way, Mom said that you can wash sneakers in the machine, so I threw mine in with the rest of my clothes. Does that sound OK?"

"Oh, no!" Jessica exclaimed.

Elizabeth shook her head. "You're supposed to wash them separately," she explained, starting to laugh. Things hadn't changed as much as she thought. The "new" Steven was very similar to the "old" one. "Do you need any help?"

"Thanks, but the day when I need help from a sixth grader is a long time away," he shouted, then dashed back down to the basement, two steps at a time.

Just then Elizabeth and Jessica heard the front door open. "I'm home!" boomed a deep voice.

Mr. Wakefield came into the kitchen, a big smile on his rugged, tanned face. With brown hair and eyes, he looked like an adult version of Steven. "How are my favorite twins?" he asked. Jessica ran over and gave him a big hug. Just as Elizabeth was about to do the same, Mr. Wakefield noticed the whirring hum coming from the basement.

He looked startled. "What's that?" he asked.

"Steven's doing his laundry," Jessica informed him.

Mr. Wakefield looked surprised. "You're kidding. All of you are turning into such responsible—"

"That's right, Dad. We really are." Jessica interrupted, in case he had changed his mind about telling them the secret.

"And that's why tonight's the night. You girls have shown me that you're old enough to keep a secret. So, do you promise not to tell anyone?"

"I promise," Elizabeth assured him, placing her right hand over her heart.

"Me, too," Jessica said.

"'Me, too' what?" her father asked.

"I promise," Jessica declared.

"Good, then we have an understanding. I'll change my clothes and say hi to your brother, and then we'll go. How does Guido's sound?"

Guido's Pizza Palace was an old family favorite, and it also had the world's best pizza. "That's a great idea," Elizabeth told her father.

"To tell you the truth, I've had so much pizza lately, it's coming out of my ears!" Jessica whispered to her sister as they raced upstairs to get ready.

"It serves you right for not bringing your lunch to school and having to eat those awful mini-pizzas in the cafeteria!" Elizabeth scolded.

For once Jessica had to agree. "You're right. Besides, it's not every day that a handsome man wants to take me out for dinner," she said with a giggle.

Elizabeth opened the door and smiled as she glanced at her neat blue-and-cream bedroom and all her familiar belongings. It wasn't long ago that she and Jessica had shared a room and constantly got into arguments about keeping it clean and how to decorate it. But all that had changed once each twin had a room of her own.

Elizabeth changed her sweater and brushed her long blond hair vigorously. After applying a dab of clear lip gloss to her mouth, she was ready to go. She walked through the adjoining bathroom to Jessica's room.

Jessica called out, "I'll be ready in a sec. Have a seat, Lizzie."

That's easier said than done, Elizabeth thought, looking around her at Jessica's pink-and-white room. Piles of clothing were on every piece of furniture. She cleared a spot on Jessica's messy bed and sat down. Then she looked around the room and wondered how Jessica ever found anything in there.

"Jess, may I have my clip back, please?" Elizabeth asked. She wanted to reclaim it before it got lost in the room's confusion. "That is, if you can find it," she joked.

"No problem," said Jessica. She went straight to the pile of clothes on her desk, reached underneath, and to Elizabeth's amazement, found the clip immediately. Jessica might not be the tidiest person in the world, Elizabeth thought, but she knew exactly where everything was.

After trying on several different outfits, Jessica still wasn't ready. "Guido's is very casual," Elizabeth reminded her. "It doesn't matter what you wear."

Looking shocked, Jessica answered, "Of course it does! It matters to *me*. I always try to look my best." Before Elizabeth could respond, Jessica changed out of her sweater and into a light blue sundress. Then she tied a purple belt around her narrow waist.

Jessica always made a point of wearing at least one purple article of clothing. She did this because she was a member of the Unicorn Club, and every girl in the club did the same. The Unicorns were very exclusive, and considered themselves to be as beautiful and special as the mythical animal of the same name. Elizabeth made no secret of the fact that she was proud *not* to be a Unicorn. She thought that the club's sole purpose was to talk about clothes and boys and to gossip about girls who weren't Unicorns.

When Jessica was finally ready, the girls ran downstairs to meet their father.

"Now, Dad?" Jessica asked excitedly.

Mr. Wakefield chuckled and said, "I'll tell you one thing, this secret is older than you girls."

Hearing this made Jessica even more impatient. "Come on, Dad, please tell us," she pleaded. "I'll die if I have to wait a second longer. . . ."

"Don't do that, it'll ruin the secret," Mr. Wakefield joked. Then he grew serious. "Ithig*l* th*ith*ig*ink th*ith*ig*is w*ith*ig*ill c*ith*ig*ome ith*ig*as ith*ig*a* s*ith*ig*urpr*ith*ig*ise.*"

"Huh?" Jessica asked, not understanding a word she'd just heard.

"What did you say?" asked Elizabeth. It sounded like a mixture of pig latin and Greek.

Their father continued, "This is a secret language called Ithig. I learned it when I was just about your age. I'm going to teach it to you, but I want it to be just between the three of us. It'll be our private way of communicating."

In a million years Elizabeth would never have guessed that this was the secret. Jessica looked a little disappointed, which was understandable since she'd been expecting something more like a trip to Europe. But as Mr. Wakefield continued to talk in Ithig, she seemed to grow more curious.

Suddenly Jessica was full of questions. "What does *ithig* mean?" Jessica asked. "How long will it take for us to learn it?"

"I promise you one thing," said Mr. Wakefield, "you'll be speaking it fluently by the time you go to bed tonight. And I'll tell you everything you need to know as soon as we get to Guido's."

Two

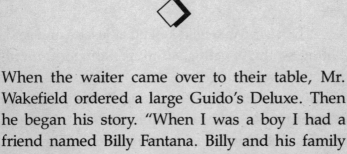

When the waiter came over to their table, Mr. Wakefield ordered a large Guido's Deluxe. Then he began his story. "When I was a boy I had a friend named Billy Fantana. Billy and his family lived across the street. We were practically inseparable. Just like you two, especially when you were little. We had a secret tree house in the woods, and we—"

"Dad," Jessica interrupted, "what about Ithig?"

"Don't worry, I'm getting there. First, I'm giving you a little background. Now then, where was I? So Billy and I . . ."

Mr. Wakefield told them that Billy had learned about Ithig from *his* father. Mr. Wakefield and Billy spoke Ithig all the time and nobody knew what they were saying. Elizabeth was fascinated. She tried to imagine her father as a little boy, and listened closely to everything he said.

But Jessica was definitely less interested. She rolled her eyes and played with her knife and fork, twirling them between her fingers like a baton. It was good practice for the Boosters, she told herself.

Then Mr. Wakefield looked at Jessica and said, "Jithigessïithigca withigants ithigto lithigearn ththigis lithigangithiguage."

Jessica looked up, thinking that she'd heard her name, but she wasn't quite sure.

Elizabeth was just as confused as her twin. She concentrated on what her father was saying. Certain sounds were familiar. And "ithig" was repeated over and over again.

"It's really very simple," Mr. Wakefield said, switching back to ordinary English.

"It doesn't sound it," said Jessica doubtfully.

"Listen closely," their father instructed them. "This is how it goes. First, each syllable of a word has its own 'ithig.' That is, you simply insert an 'ithig' *inside* each syllable. For example, let's take the word twin. In Ithig, it would be 'twithigin.'"

Elizabeth stared at her father, trying to follow what he was saying.

"Now you try it. How would you say the word girl in Ithig?"

After a few moments Elizabeth answered, "I think it would be '*githigirl*.'"

"Very good!" exclaimed Mr. Wakefield. He continued, "But words of two letters or less, like I, it, and am, *start* with ithig. Ithig*I*, ithig*it*, ithig*am*, and so on. Basically, that's the secret. Give it a try, Jess."

"Yes, try," urged Elizabeth. "I mean, *Y*ithig*es*, *tr*ithig*y*!"

"*G*ithig*ood w*ithig*ork, L*ithig*iz*." Mr. Wakefield laughed and patted her on the back.

"*Th*ithig*anks, D*ithig*ad*," Elizabeth replied.

"This was supposed to be between the three of us!" Jessica protested. Elizabeth could already speak this new language and she could barely understand it. It wasn't fair!

"Honey, you'll pick this up in no time," her father reassured her.

"Think of how much fun it's going to be!" Elizabeth exclaimed. "Everyone will go absolutely crazy. Think how upset Lila will be!"

Lila Fowler was a Unicorn and a good friend of Jessica's. She was the daughter of one of the wealthiest men in Sweet Valley. Elizabeth thought she was a big snob and spoiled rotten. She really wasn't concerned with what Lila thought, but she knew that her sister cared a great deal.

Jessica took a moment to concentrate, trying to remember the rules to Ithig. Just then she saw Caroline Pearce walk into the restaurant with her mother. Caroline wrote the gossip column for the *Sweet Valley Sixers* and was known as the biggest blabbermouth in school. She had very long red hair and always wore her shirts buttoned all the way up to the top.

Jessica blurted out, "*Caro*lithig*ine Pearce*ithig ithig*is here*ithig!"

Mr. Wakefield smiled at her effort, even though it was a little mixed up. "At first everyone has a little trouble with Ithig," he commented. Then he asked Elizabeth if she knew the correct way to say "Caroline Pearce is here" in Ithig.

After thinking it over for a moment, Elizabeth replied, "*Ca*rithigo*lithig*ine *P*ithig*earce* ithig*is h*ithi*gere*!"

"Very good!" Then he turned to Jessica and repeated the rules. "You see, every syllable gets an 'ithig.' With short words, put the 'ithig' first."

"But Caroline really *is* here," Jessica insisted.

Elizabeth looked over her shoulder. Sure enough, Caroline was standing there.

"Pretend you don't see her," Jessica whispered. "I don't want her coming over here. She's always sticking her nose in where it doesn't belong."

At that moment Caroline spotted them, waved, and started walking toward their table. "Ithig*oh* ithig*no!*" cried Jessica.

"Shhh," Elizabeth urged, putting her finger to her lips.

When Caroline reached their table, she asked suspiciously, "Did I hear something strange going on at this table?"

Jessica smiled sweetly. "You heard us speaking a different language."

"Oh, really?" Caroline said, her eyes widening in surprise. "What is it? French? Spanish?"

"I'm sorry, Caroline, but I can't say. It's a secret language that's only between the three of us," Jessica told her.

But Caroline wasn't about to let the subject drop. "Why is it a secret?" she persisted.

"This is sort of a family matter, Caroline," Mr.

Wakefield said. "You must have secrets in your family. . . ."

"None like this," Caroline retorted, and walked toward the next table.

"Ithig*I* ithig*am* pr*i*thig*oud* ithig*of* *y*ithig*ou*, *J*ithig*ess*, *f*ithig*or* *n*ithig*ot* *t*ithig*elli*thig*ing*," Mr. Wakefield said to Jessica.

Just then the waiter appeared, carrying a steaming pizza high above his shoulder. He placed it on the table and suggested they let it cool off for a few minutes before they started eating. But Jessica, who rarely paid attention to advice, immediately pulled a slice toward her and took a bite. "Ouch!" she cried.

"Jessica, why didn't you listen to the waiter?" Elizabeth scolded. "You have the patience of a flea!" She quickly pushed a glass of water toward Jessica.

"Ithig*I* ithig*am* *s*ithig*orry,*" apologized Jessica after downing the whole glass of water in three gulps.

"Pretty good, Jess," Mr. Wakefield commented. "Just remember, each syllable has its own 'ithig.' If a word has more than one syllable, you continue in the same manner for each."

Jessica corrected herself, "Ithig*I* ithig*am* *s*ithi-gorri*thigy*."

Mr. Wakefield smiled. "Both of you are very quick learners. It took me days to get the hang of this."

"*Thi*thig*anks, D*ithig*ad*," said Elizabeth.

"Ithig*we l*ithig*ove th*ithig*is se*ithigcri*thiget!*" Jessica declared.

"Ithig*I k*nithig*ew y*ithig*ou w*ithig*ould*," Mr. Wakefield said with a grin.

Three

◇

The next morning Elizabeth sat at the kitchen table eating a bowlful of cereal while Jessica painted purple stripes on each of her pink fingernails. Although Elizabeth thought the end result looked a little ridiculous, the process was fascinating. With deft fingers Jessica applied each stroke. She dipped the brush in the polish, wiped off the excess on the side of the bottle, then made a single, careful line lengthwise down the nail. She repeated the exact same procedure for each fingernail.

"You're a real artist when it comes to fingernail painting," Elizabeth told her sister.

"*Thithigank yithigou, bithigig sithigis*," Jessica said with a smile. She waved her hands back and forth and started to blow on her fingertips.

Steven sauntered into the kitchen with his books under his arm. He took one look at Jessica's outstretched hands and made a face. "Oh boy!" he exclaimed. "What happened? Did you get your fingers slammed in the door?"

"No one asked you, Steven," Jessica snapped.

"Too bad," he remarked.

Mr. Wakefield came into the kitchen, briefcase in hand. "I'm in a hurry," he said, "Anybody need a ride?"

"Sure," said Steven.

"What about you two?" Mr. Wakefield asked the twins.

"Thanks, Dad, but I'd rather walk," said Elizabeth.

Jessica nodded in agreement and said, "Ithig*we* bithig*oth* withig*ant* ithig*to* withig*alk*. . . ."

Putting his fingers to his lips, Mr. Wakefield said, "Shhh. Remember, this is a secret."

Steven shook his head and looked confused. "This family's getting really weird," he said, following Mr. Wakefield out the door.

As soon as they left, Jessica broke out laughing. "The best part about Ithig," she said, "is that Steven doesn't know it!"

"Well, he will soon if he keeps hearing you

speak it," Elizabeth warned. She got up and said, "Ready?"

Jessica lightly touched her fingertip to see if it was dry. "Lizzie, would you do me a favor and carry my books?" she asked. "My nails are still damp, and I don't want them to smudge."

Elizabeth had the feeling that once again Jessica was trying to con her. But before she could give her an answer, Mrs. Wakefield walked in, yawning. She had on her favorite terry robe, and her pretty blue eyes looked as if they weren't quite awake yet.

"Morning, Mom," Elizabeth said brightly.

"*Mithigornithiging, Mithigom,*" said Jessica.

Mrs. Wakefield looked surprised. "Is that the language your father was talking about?" she asked.

"*Yithiges ithigit ithigis!*" Jessica declared with delight.

"Oh, my! Dad taught you that?"

"Yes. But the thing is, Mom, it's sort of a secret just between Dad and us. You see, when Dad was our age he had this friend—." Elizabeth began. She didn't want to hurt her mother's feelings.

"Honey, there's no need to explain. I understand completely. I think it's wonderful that you girls and your father have something private and special."

"Thanks, Mom. You're terrific." Elizabeth turned to her sister and said, "Are your nails dry yet? I really don't want to carry your books. I have enough of my own." Jessica looked surprised. She wasn't used to being turned down by her sister.

At this point Mrs. Wakefield noticed Jessica's hands. "How interesting," she commented. "I don't believe I've ever seen anything quite like that."

"Thanks, Mom. I came up with this design all by myself."

"Are you girls hungry?" Mrs. Wakefield asked. "Can I fix you some breakfast?"

"No, thanks. We're in a hurry," Jessica answered. She turned to Elizabeth. "*Lithigets githi-get githigoithiging.*"

Elizabeth followed her to the door, surprised to find that Jessica had agreed to carry her own books. "Bye, Mom. Have a good day."

"*Githigoodbithigye, Mithigom,*" Jessica sang out.

Elizabeth and Jessica strolled down the tree-lined streets of Sweet Valley, California, a town which both twins thought was the most perfect place on earth. As always, the sun was shining in a blue sky that was dotted with only the tiniest puffs of clouds.

"Ithig*I* withig*on*dithig*er* wh*ithigat ev*ithig*e-ry*ithig*one* withig*ill th*ithig*ink* wh*ithigen th*ithig*ey* h*ithig*ear* ithig*us*?" said Jessica.

"Remember, Jess, this is supposed to be a secret," Elizabeth said.

"I know that," Jessica said indignantly.

"Well, then, I don't think we should blab it all over school."

"Lizzie! I have no intention of doing that. Ithig*I* c*ithigan* k*ithig*eep* ithig*a se*ithig*crithig*et* ithig*as* withig*ell* ithig*as an*ithig*yithig*one!*"

Elizabeth looked doubtful, and Jessica started to get angry. "Ithig*I* withig*ould* ne*ithigevithiger* ithig*go* b*ithigack* ithig*on* ithig*my* withig*ord!*" she declared loudly. "*Wh*ithig*at* ithig*do y*ithig*ou—*"

Just then a familiar-sounding voice called out their names. Elizabeth and Jessica stopped and turned around. It was Amy Sutton, one of Elizabeth's friends. "Wait up!" she called, running toward them.

"What's going on?" Amy asked when she caught up with the twins. Her pale blue eyes were bright and curious.

"Not much," Elizabeth answered. "What's going on with you, Amy?"

Amy was a smart girl, and she was also very direct. "I thought I just heard Jessica say something weird."

"Oh, Jessica was just fooling around," Elizabeth told her. But she felt terrible about fibbing. Aside from Jessica, Amy was her best friend, and Elizabeth hated not being able to tell her about Ithig.

Amy pressed on. "Are you sure? I could've sworn I heard—"

"Well, you didn't!" snapped Jessica, cutting her off.

"You don't have to get nasty," Amy snapped back. Before Elizabeth could apologize for her sister's rudeness, Amy said, "I'll see you later, Elizabeth." Then she took off and ran down the block.

Jessica turned to Elizabeth with a big smile on her face. "Aren't you proud of me? I didn't say a word about the secret."

Elizabeth couldn't believe what she was hearing. "Proud of you? I'm furious with you!" she cried. "How could you speak to Amy that way?"

"What do you mean?" Jessica asked, looking confused. "First you don't want me to speak Ithig in front of anyone. Then you get angry at me when I don't. . . ."

They were half a block away from school, and Elizabeth didn't want to start an argument. Already she could see groups of students milling around on the lawn in front of the sprawling brick building. "Let's just forget about Ithig for now," she suggested. "We can talk about this later."

"Fine," Jessica agreed.

As they approached the entrance to Sweet Valley Middle School, a group of Jessica's Unicorn friends came over to the twins. Lila Fowler was at the head of the group, and she looked upset.

"Hi, Lila," Jessica called out cheerfully, waving to her friend.

But Lila just tossed her shoulder-length brown hair and flashed a cunning smile. "There's something we want to discuss with you," she said.

"What's that?" Jessica asked.

"Caroline told us that you two have a secret language," Lila said.

Jessica giggled nervously. "That girl is always saying all sorts of things that aren't true," she said, trying to make light of the situation.

"So she made this whole thing up?" Lila asked suspiciously.

Jessica looked down at the ground. Then she glanced at Elizabeth, clearly looking for help. But Elizabeth just shrugged her shoulders. In a very small voice, Jessica answered, "No."

"Ha! She was right! How could you tell Caroline about this first? This is a huge insult to the Unicorns!" Lila hissed, sounding angrier with each word she spoke. Her brown eyes looked as if they were on fire.

"I didn't tell Caroline anything!" Jessica cried in a desperate attempt to explain herself. "She just happened to overhear us speaking. . . ."

"Speaking what?" Lila pressed on.

"Yeah, speaking what?" Janet Howell chimed in. Janet was Lila's first cousin and the president of the Unicorn Club.

"Tell us, Jessica," insisted Ellen Riteman, who could be just as demanding as Lila.

All of the Unicorns were pressing in on Jessica. It was a difficult position to be in, and she didn't know how to get out of it. If she told them about Ithig, she'd be breaking the promise she'd made to her father and Elizabeth. But how could she keep a secret from the entire Unicorn Club?

Elizabeth spoke up, coming to her sister's defense. "It's a special language that our father taught us. He made us promise not to tell anyone," she explained simply. As she spoke, Elizabeth noticed Amy sitting on a nearby bench. It was clear from the look on her face that she'd heard everything.

Elizabeth went over to her friend, but Amy immediately got up and started walking away. "Amy!" Elizabeth yelled, but Amy didn't turn around. Elizabeth ran after her and called her name again.

Finally, Amy faced her. "Elizabeth, you lied to me," she said, her lips trembling.

"I'm sorry, Amy. I didn't mean—"

"You lied to me," Amy repeated. "I asked what you and Jessica were up to, and you said nothing. And then you had the nerve to admit everything to those dumb Unicorns." Amy pushed her straight blond hair out of her face. Elizabeth could see tears welling up in her eyes.

"Amy, I never meant to hurt you," Elizabeth said honestly. "Let me explain. You see, my dad taught us this special language and made us promise to keep it a secret, you know what I mean? So, last night at Guido's, Caroline overheard us speaking it, and now she's telling everyone. The only reason I said anything about it to the Unicorns was because they were giving Jessica such a hard time. You know how awful they can be. . . ."

Just then the bell rang. Elizabeth put her arm around her friend and said, "We can talk more later, OK?"

Amy wiped her moist eyes with the edge of her sleeve. "OK," she said with a tentative smile.

Four

◇

It was lunchtime, and Elizabeth was on her way to the cafeteria. Someone tapped her on the shoulder, and she wheeled around and saw Amy.

"I've been looking all over for you," Amy told her.

"I had to see Mr. Bowman and give him the master for next week's issue," Elizabeth said. Mr. Bowman was their English teacher and supervisor of the *Sweet Valley Sixers*.

"Do you want to eat lunch together?" asked Amy.

"Sure," Elizabeth replied enthusiastically. After what happened that morning, Elizabeth was pleased to see Amy acting like her old self again.

As they walked down the hall, Elizabeth said

to her friend, "I'm sorry about what happened earlier. I never thought that a silly secret could cause so much trouble. It doesn't seem that Lila is ever going to forgive Jessica."

"Why is it silly?" Amy asked.

Elizabeth hesitated for a moment. "It just is. If you knew the secret, I'm sure you'd agree."

"It all sounds so mysterious," Amy remarked. "You and Jessica must be having a lot of fun with this language."

Elizabeth thought it would be best to change the subject. "We need more articles for the next *Sixers*. I was hoping you'd have some ideas."

But Amy wasn't about to let the subject drop. "Liz, since you don't want to tell me the secret, maybe you could just say something in the language. . . ."

Elizabeth shook her head. "It's not that I don't want to tell you. The point is, I gave my word that I wouldn't."

"How about if you write it down?" Amy persisted. "Then you really wouldn't be telling me, would you?"

Though she was half joking, Elizabeth knew that Amy was also half serious. "Amy, can't we forget about this?"

"Couldn't you at least tell me the name of the language?"

Elizabeth was growing annoyed. "I don't understand why you're making such a big deal out of this," she said. "It's not like you."

Amy's mouth grew tight and she appeared to be getting upset all over again. Her tone became angry as she looked Elizabeth in the eye, and said, "Why? I'll tell you why. We're supposed to be best friends, and best friends aren't supposed to have secrets from each other. Sometimes I think that you already have a best friend, and her name is Jessica!"

Elizabeth was speechless. She had no idea that Amy was the slightest bit jealous of Jessica. "That's not true!" she cried.

Amy just stared at Elizabeth, a hurt look in her eyes. Elizabeth didn't know what to say. "I guess I sort of have two best friends," she muttered finally.

"Oh, yeah? Well, from now on you only have one!" With that Amy stomped away.

Elizabeth stood in the hall in a state of shock, too stunned to follow the crowd of students heading for the cafeteria. She'd never known Amy to be so unreasonable.

"Hey, Elizabeth, are you coming to lunch?" a friendly voice called out.

Elizabeth turned around and saw Julie Porter and Mary Robinson waiting for her. "Uh, yes, in a minute. Why don't you go ahead and I'll meet you there," Elizabeth told them. At the moment she was too upset even to think about eating. Maybe going outside for some fresh air would help.

As she walked downstairs she heard two girls arguing on the landing above her. Elizabeth couldn't see them, but their voices were loud and clear, and very familiar. Jessica and Lila Fowler.

"If you don't tell me your secret, I'll never speak to you again for the rest of my life!" Lila shouted.

"How can I? I promised my father and sister!" Jessica pleaded.

"That's not my problem," Lila said nastily. She could be very unpleasant when things didn't go her way.

Then Elizabeth heard a door slam and a whimpering sound, like someone crying. She ran up the stairs as fast as she could. Jessica was sitting on the steps with her head in her hands, sobbing quietly. Elizabeth put her arm around her sister's shoulders.

Through her tears Jessica said, "How did this happen? I didn't do anything to hurt anyone."

Elizabeth understood completely. She felt exactly the same way. Their closest friends had suddenly turned against them for no good reason.

"What are we going to do?" Jessica asked after she had calmed down.

"Let's first go eat lunch," she suggested, hoping that perhaps some food would make them feel better.

Jessica stood up and straightened her skirt. She ran her fingers through her hair and pulled up her socks. Then she pulled a tissue from her purse and dabbed her damp eyes. "Lizzie, do I look OK?" she asked.

"You look absolutely *fi*thig*ine*!" Elizabeth said, putting on her brightest smile. Jessica broke into a wide grin and gave her a hug.

They raced downstairs to the cafeteria. At the top of her lungs, Jessica yelled, "Ithig*I'm st*ithig*ar-v*ithig*ing*!"

Jessica hadn't brought her lunch to school, so Elizabeth waited with her on the cafeteria line. Then they walked out to the seating area.

Carrying her tray, Jessica glanced at the table

where the Unicorn Club always sat. She was surprised to see that Amy and Caroline, who weren't in the club, were sitting right at the center of the long table. Jessica felt a pang of sadness. The Unicorns hadn't even saved a seat for her.

Elizabeth was also surprised to see Amy with the Unicorns. She was chatting and giggling as if she sat with the club every day. Elizabeth knew Amy didn't like spending much time in the company of the Unicorns. *What is Amy up to*? she asked herself.

Trying to ignore the Unicorns, Jessica scanned the room, looking for a place to sit. The only free seats were at a table not far from the Unicorns, with people she and her sister hardly knew. Having no alternative, they went over and sat down.

Jessica ate her sandwich quickly and nervously, while Elizabeth just nibbled at hers. She overheard their names being mentioned at the Unicorn table, but tried not to pay attention.

Jessica, however, became enraged. She shot a dirty look across the room, but no one seemed to notice. They were too busy whispering among themselves. Then she got an idea. "I have the perfect way to get back at them," she told Elizabeth.

Jessica pushed her wispy bangs out of her face and cleared her throat. "*Thithigis withigill mithigake thithigem angithigry*," she said at the top of her voice. But the girls at the Unicorn table still didn't pay any attention to her. Raising her voice even louder, Jessica continued, "*Nithigow yithigou sithigay sithigomethithiging, Lithigiz*."

"Later," Elizabeth insisted.

Jessica's scheme wasn't working. The people sitting nearby stared at her, but still no one at the Unicorn table even bothered to look up. They just continued to whisper as if they hadn't heard a thing out of the ordinary. It made Jessica furious.

She stood up and went directly over to the Unicorns table. As she approached, the whispering stopped. All the girls at the table turned their heads away and pointedly ignored her.

Jessica had never felt more humiliated in her life. There was no way she was going to let the Unicorns get away with it, she decided.

"How long is this going to last?" she asked, trying to stay calm.

"Till you tell us the secret to your language," Lila said flatly.

"I can't, Lila. Do you expect me to break the promise I made to my father and sister?"

Lila just stared back at her. None of the other girls breathed a word. Apparently that's exactly what they did expect.

Five

◇

Elizabeth was rummaging through her locker, getting ready to go home for the day, when Amy passed by. "Hey, Amy," she called.

"Yes?" Amy replied, a distinct chill in her voice.

Trying to ease the tension between them, Elizabeth said, "Um, I was wondering . . . would you like to come over today? Jessica won't be there—she has a Unicorn meeting. I thought maybe you and I could talk."

"Sorry, I'm busy," Amy said curtly, going over to her locker.

"Well, how about tomorrow?" Elizabeth persisted, following Amy as she walked away.

"I have plans," Amy replied.

"Amy, don't you think you're being a bit unreasonable?" Elizabeth said.

But before Amy had a chance to reply, Lila Fowler came breezing around the corner, a mischievous grin on her face. She ran directly over to Amy and shrieked, "Have I got news for you! I just spoke to my father and he's arranged for Chris Crosby to be the star at the benefit for the hospital. It's going to be at my house on Saturday, and Daddy told me to invite all of my friends. I hope you can make it, Amy."

"Make it? Are you kidding? Chris Crosby is my favorite tennis player in the world! I absolutely adore him! You mean, I'm actually going to see him in person?" Amy was practically screaming with delight.

Lila glanced at Elizabeth, but made no effort to include her in the conversation. Elizabeth went to her locker and pretended she was looking for something. She was suspicious about Lila's sudden interest in Amy. Everyone knew that they only talked to each other because of the Boosters.

"I have so much to do," Lila was saying. "I have to send the invitations, figure out what I'm going to wear . . . do you want to help me, Amy?"

"Sure. I'd love to," Amy replied.

"Great," Lila said. Then she lowered her voice and added, "By the way, do you think I should invite Jessica and Elizabeth? I mean, since they won't tell us their secret."

Elizabeth shut her locker with a loud bang and wheeled around just in time to see Lila link her arm through Amy's as they walked down the hall. Amy was talking, but Elizabeth couldn't hear what she was saying. She wondered if Amy was agreeing with Lila's spiteful plan.

Elizabeth didn't mind missing a party. Missing the chance to see Chris Crosby didn't bother her either. But it broke her heart that she was losing her best friend, especially to someone as phony as Lila.

When Elizabeth walked outside, she was surprised to see Jessica sitting alone on the steps. "Hi," she said. "I thought you had a Unicorn meeting today."

"It was cancelled," Jessica said with a frown. "Besides, I'm not attending another meeting until they start acting nicer to me. I couldn't believe that scene at lunch."

"I know what you mean," Elizabeth replied. She sighed sympathetically. "Amy won't even talk to me."

As they walked across the lawn, Elizabeth didn't mention Lila's party, fearing the news might send Jessica into a rage. But just as they were leaving the school grounds, Amy and Lila strolled right across their path, talking loudly. Lila was saying, "This is going to be the greatest party ever. The twins will turn absolutely green!"

When Jessica heard the word "party," she stopped in her tracks. "Lila," she called, "what were you just saying?"

"I'm sorry, Jessica, but I can't tell you. It's a secret," Lila answered haughtily as she and Amy faced the twins.

"Did you say something about a party?" asked Jessica.

"Oh, you mean the one I'm having this weekend? It's going to be very special," Lila bragged.

"Why is that?" Jessica asked.

"Only because Chris Crosby is going to be there, and my dad's arranged for him to play a match in the afternoon. It'll be a big event but *I'm* having my own private party. . . ."

"Chris Crosby?" Jessica gasped, her mouth falling open.

Lila continued, "Yes, it's a benefit, and all the proceeds are going to the hospital. The adults have to make donations, but my friends can come for free. Of course, I'm only inviting my closest friends." Then she paused, grinned maliciously, and added, "I guess that means you two won't be coming."

"Lila, how could you do this to me?" Jessica demanded, outraged.

"Well, look what you two did to her," Amy declared.

Elizabeth looked her friend directly in the eye. "Amy, I didn't hurt your feelings on purpose," she said. "If I could tell the secret, you'd be the first person I'd—"

"Ha!" Lila interrupted. "Don't believe that for one minute, Amy. Now they'll get a taste of their own medicine and see how it feels! Come on, Amy, we have lots to do," she said, grabbing Amy's arm.

Amy looked at Elizabeth, but followed Lila. As they walked away, Lila looked over her shoulder and said to Jessica, "If you tell me your secret, maybe I'll change my mind about inviting you to the party." Then she and Amy hurried off together.

"Can you believe this?" cried Jessica. "What are we going to do?"

Elizabeth just shook her head.

The twins walked home in silence. They didn't even feel like speaking Ithig. "I think this has been the worst day of my life," Jessica declared.

"Don't worry. I'm sure this will blow over," Elizabeth said hopefully. "In a week no one will even remember that we had a secret."

"Maybe," Jessica said, not sounding convinced. "But I'll just die if I can't go to that party. Everyone's going to be there. I wish we'd never even heard of Ithig!"

Later that afternoon, when Mr. Wakefield came home and walked into the kitchen, the first thing he said was, "*Dithigid yithigou kithigeep ithigour seithigcrithiget?*"

"*Yithiges, Dithigad,*" Elizabeth answered with a groan.

"*Ithigis sithigomethithiging writhigong?*" Mr. Wakefield asked, sounding concerned.

"*Withigell . . .*" Jessica started to say, but Elizabeth immediately cut her off.

"*Ithigno,*" she said flatly. She didn't want to spoil her father's good mood. Maybe she and Jessica could figure out a solution to their problem on their own.

"I've got a few calls to make," Mr. Wakefield announced. "Ithig*we* c*ith*ig*an t*ith*ig*alk l*ith*ig*a*t*ith*ig*er*," he said as he left the room.

Steven walked in, his books under his arm. He dropped them on the counter and went directly to the refrigerator. He grabbed as many things as he could hold in one arm, carried them over to the table, and started making a sandwich.

"Hey, did you hear about Lila's party?" he asked his sisters, spreading mayonnaise on a slice of bread.

"Yes," Jessica sighed.

"It sounds really great. I can't wait to go," he said.

"Since when are you going to a party of Lila's?" Jessica asked, surprised. Most of the time Steven made fun of Lila.

"Since she started inviting famous tennis players. This is one party that I'm definitely not going to miss."

"So, how did you manage to get yourself invited?" she prodded her brother.

"Lila just found me after school and invited

me. I guess she wanted to have some older men there for decoration," he joked.

"*I* guess she wanted to rub it in some more," Jessica muttered under her breath.

"What did you say?" Steven asked.

"Never mind," said Jessica. "It's just that Elizabeth and I aren't going."

Steven looked surprised. "What's the matter? You always go to Lila's parties. Did you have a fight or something?" he asked.

"It's a long story," Jessica said wearily.

"Well, I think you should try and make up," Steven advised, "because this is supposed to be the party of the year. They're having TV stars, photographers—"

"TV stars? Who?" she asked, her lower lip trembling.

"Lila said someone named Brett Carter's going to be there—"

"Brett Carter! I adore Brett Carter," Jessica screamed. He was one of her favorite soap opera stars. "I can't miss this party. I just can't!" Jessica cried. Then she turned and ran upstairs, bursting into tears.

Six

◇

The staff of *Sweet Valley Sixers* was assembling their latest issue in Mr. Bowman's classroom. Amy and Sophia Rizzo collated the freshly mimeographed pages, Pamela Jacobson stapled, and Mary Robinson stacked the copies neatly. Julie Porter counted them and handed the finished copies to Elizabeth.

While they worked, the girls chatted and caught up on recent happenings. No one seemed to notice that Amy and Elizabeth weren't talking to each other.

"I've got some real exciting news," Mary reported. Mary was in the seventh grade, but she sometimes volunteered to help out the *Sixers* staff.

"What's that?" Elizabeth asked eagerly.

Mary put down the papers in her hand. "My mom's got a new boyfriend," she said, her eyes sparkling brightly. "She's been seeing a lot of him. . . ."

"How does your mother feel about him?" Elizabeth asked, hoping that Mrs. Robinson had found a nice man. She was a divorcée and new to Sweet Valley, and Elizabeth imagined that it was lonely for her.

"She says they're getting serious," Mary said with a big smile.

"That's great!" everyone chorused. Though they'd never discussed it, Elizabeth suspected that Mary would be thrilled to have a father. She'd spent most of her life in foster homes, as Mary Giaccio. It was only recently that she became reunited with her real mother and became Mary Robinson.

Mr. Bowman strolled into the room. "How's it going?" he asked with a wink.

Pointing to the tall stack of finished *Sixers*, Elizabeth replied, "We're almost done."

"Does anyone have ideas for the next issue?" Mr. Bowman asked, sitting down at his desk. "I don't think we have enough articles."

"Chris Crosby is going to be appearing in Sweet Valley," Amy replied eagerly. "It's going to be a benefit for the hospital, and it's taking place at the Fowlers'. I think it would make a great story."

"So do I," said Mr. Bowman, stroking his chin. "Are any of you going?" he questioned them.

"I am," everyone said in unison—everyone except Elizabeth.

"Well, who do you think should get this assignment?" Mr. Bowman asked Elizabeth.

Elizabeth paused for a moment to think about the question. She was sure that Amy would love the job, but when she looked over at her, Amy lowered her eyes nervously. Elizabeth suspected that Amy thought she wasn't going to be chosen because of their argument. But Elizabeth wouldn't do that to Amy.

"I think Amy should do it. After all, she knows more about sports than any of us," offered Elizabeth.

Amy broke into a smile. "Thank you," she said, though she didn't look at Elizabeth.

"Fine. Any other ideas for articles?" Mr. Bowman asked.

"How about a story on the Sweet Valley Symphony? My father could arrange an interview," suggested Julie, whose father was a professional musician.

"That's a great idea!" Elizabeth said. "You're such a good piano player. I think you'd be the perfect person to do this piece."

Julie smiled shyly. "I'll talk to my dad tonight," she said.

"That's a great idea, Julie. Any others? What about you, Elizabeth?" Mr. Bowman asked.

"Um, uh, not really . . ." Elizabeth admitted apologetically. Most of the time she had plenty of ideas, but now she was still upset over her argument with Amy. "But I'll come up with something for our next meeting," she promised.

"Then we'll call it a day," announced Mr. Bowman, handing a stack of papers to each girl.

Usually Amy and Elizabeth distributed copies of the *Sixers* on the first floor, leaving stacks in the sixth-grade homerooms, and the other girls brought them to the cafeteria and auditorium. But today Amy started to follow Julie out of the room. "We'll take care of the cafeteria," Julie called as they left.

Though Elizabeth tried not to show that anything was wrong, inside she felt it strongly. She missed Amy's company more and more. But what could she do? If she made up with Amy by telling her secret, she would be going back on her word. She wished Amy would try to understand. . . .

Out in the corridor with a stack of *Sixers* under her arm, Elizabeth walked down the quiet hall. Most of the kids had already left for the day, and a lot of the classrooms were already locked. From where she stood, Elizabeth saw that the music room was still open and the lights on. As she headed in that direction she heard loud voices coming from within. It sounded like a party. She wondered if Mr. Garvin, her music teacher, knew about it.

Elizabeth poked her head in the door and discovered a group of teachers standing around Mr. Garvin's desk with small paper cups in their hands. They were all laughing and smiling. Feeling surprised and out of place, Elizabeth stood in the doorway without saying a word.

Mr. Garvin was the first to notice her. "Elizabeth! How long have you been here?" he asked, a big grin on his face.

"I just came to drop off the *Sixers*. I didn't mean to interrupt," Elizabeth said apologetically. She plopped a stack of papers down on the desk nearest the door. But as she turned to leave, Mr.

Garvin stopped her. "Please stay for a little while."

On Mr. Garvin's desk Elizabeth noticed a bottle of champagne, a carton of orange juice, and a stack of paper cups. "What's going on?" she asked.

"We're celebrating the birth of Mr. Garvin's first baby," Mrs. Arnette announced.

"Mr. Garvin had a baby?" said Elizabeth, surprised. She didn't even know he was married.

"I think it was his wife that had the baby," Mr. Nydick, the white-haired man who taught social studies, said with a chuckle.

"That's right. This morning at thirteen minutes after eleven," added Mr. Garvin, shaking his head as if he still couldn't believe it had actually happened.

"Gee, Mr. Garvin, congratulations!" said Elizabeth. She had always liked Mr. Garvin, and she was sure he'd make a great dad.

"Here," said Ms. Wyler as she handed Elizabeth a cup of orange juice. "Let's drink a toast to young Michael Jay Garvin. Here's to his health and happiness." She held up her cup and took a sip.

"Michael? I like that name," Elizabeth said to Mr. Garvin. She was so happy for her teacher that for a moment she forgot all about the trouble she was having with Amy.

When Elizabeth arrived home that day, a letter was waiting on the hall table. The envelope was addressed to her. She tore it open excitedly and read:

Dith*ig*ear El*i*thig*izi*thig*abi*thig*eth*,
Y*i*thig*ou* ithig*are inv*ithig*iti*thig*ed* ithig*to*
ithig*a ti*thig*enni*thig*is* p*i*thig*arti*thig*y* . . .

It went on to give the date and time of the Fowlers' tennis benefit and was signed by Lila—all in Ithig! How in the world had Lila learned to write in Ithig?

It didn't take long for Elizabeth to realize that Jessica must have told Lila the secret. How else could Lila have learned the language?

Elizabeth ran up to her room and waited for her sister to return home. Too upset to read or write, she threw herself on her bed and just lay there, staring at the ceiling. When Jessica got home, Elizabeth was really going to let her have it!

Soon Elizabeth heard her sister's footsteps on the stairs. Whistling and humming to herself, Jessica sounded as if she were in a good mood. *Too good*, Elizabeth thought angrily.

Sticking her head in Elizabeth's doorway, Jessica said cheerfully. "Hi, Lizzie. How was your day?"

"Not good," Elizabeth replied. She got up and waved the invitation. "What do you know about this, Miss Benedict-Arnold Wakefield?"

"I don't know what you're talking about," Jessica answered innocently. She took the card from Elizabeth and read it. Her cheeks paled. "I can't believe it!" she exclaimed. "This time Lila's gone too far. . . ."

"Why is it Lila's fault?" Elizabeth said sternly. "You're the one who squealed!"

"But Lila told me she wouldn't tell anyone!" Jessica said defensively. "She promised that if I told her the secret, she wouldn't breathe a word. Now look what she's done! I never should have trusted her!" Jessica cried.

"What about yourself?" Elizabeth demanded. "You blabbed our secret, didn't you?"

"Well, not exactly," said Jessica, a thoughtful look crossing her face. "I had to do something, Lizzie. Our best friends were turning against us! I couldn't just sit back and let that happen."

"You just wanted to get invited to Lila's party!" Elizabeth cried angrily. "Isn't that right, Jess? You told her just so you could go to her stupid party!"

"Don't be so dramatic, Lizzie. You're making too much of this—"

"We promised. Or don't you remember?"

"Of course I do," Jessica insisted.

"Then admit what you did was wrong!" Elizabeth demanded.

"Why was it so wrong?" Jessica asked innocently. "You got invited to the party, didn't you? So what's the big deal?"

"You broke your word. You went back on a promise. Doesn't that mean anything to you?" she said, her voice rising.

"Sure it does. But so do friends and having fun," Jessica cried, her lower lip trembling. Large tears started to run down her smooth cheeks. "You don't have to act so high and mighty!" she cried out.

"Hey, what's going on up there?" Mr. Wakefield called from the foot of the stairs.

Clearing her throat, Jessica jumped up and called back, "Nothing, Dad." Then she closed her sister's door.

But a second later they heard a knock. "May I come in?" Mr. Wakefield asked.

"Sure, Dad," Elizabeth called as Jessica quickly wiped her eyes.

Mr. Wakefield walked in and said, "I could hear you two all the way in the den. What's going on? Maybe I can help."

At first neither Jessica nor Elizabeth said a word. Then Jessica, who had been trying to act as if nothing were wrong, could not hold back her tears any longer. Mr. Wakefield immediately went over and put his arm around her. "There, there, honey," he said comfortingly. "Why don't you tell me what the problem is."

At this, Jessica broke down and started to sob uncontrollably. "Oh, Dad, whatever I do, it's always wrong."

"What do you mean?" her father said with concern.

Between sobs Jessica told him the whole story. "First Lila and Amy found out about our language, and they got really upset with me and Elizabeth because we wouldn't break our promise and tell them the secret," Jessica explained. "Then Lila decided not to invite us to this really great party that she's having. I'm sure even you've heard about it. You know, the benefit the Fowlers are having with Chris Crosby—"

"Yes, Steven did mention something about that," Mr. Wakefield interrupted.

"Anyway, the only way Lizzie and I could get invited was to teach Lila how to speak Ithig," Jessica explained.

"So what did you do?" Mr. Wakefield asked.

"I told her the secret," Jessica answered softly. "But only after she promised not to tell anyone," she added.

"I see. And how do you feel about this, Elizabeth?" Mr. Wakefield asked.

"I think it would have been nice if she told me that she planned on letting Lila know. I mean, we all three promised that we wouldn't tell, right?" Elizabeth looked at her father for an answer.

Mr. Wakefield shook his head. "I'm sorry Ithig has caused such problems for you girls," he said. "I certainly never intended that. There's nothing good about something that causes this kind of trouble between sisters and friends."

"Then you think I did the right thing?" Jessica asked eagerly.

"Well, not exactly," he said. "But I think I understand. However, I do think you owe your sister an apology. You should have told her first, and me, too, for that matter. It really wasn't fair."

Jessica turned to her sister and said in her most sincere voice, "I'm sorry Lizzie. What I did was wrong, but I just wanted everything to be all right again. Please forgive me." She gave her sister a big hug and added, "I promise I'll never squeal on a secret again."

Knowing her twin as well as she did, Elizabeth wasn't totally convinced of this. But she smiled and forgave her nonetheless. She could never stay angry at Jessica for long. And maybe now that the secret was out, life would start returning to normal.

Seven

◇

"Oh, Lizzie, it's going to be so much fun! I wish
you'd come," Jessica urged. She was browsing
through her sister's closet, looking for a sweater to
wear with her new dress.

"No, thanks," Elizabeth said firmly. "I'm going to spend a quiet day alone, trying to write a
story."

"But you can write a story any time," she protested. "How often will you have the chance to see
Chris Crosby?" She pulled Elizabeth's yellow car-
digan off its hanger. "Can I borrow this one?" she
asked.

Elizabeth nodded. "I'm not going to Lila's
party. I just don't want to have anything to do
with her," she said.

"OK, have it your way. But I think you're

making a big mistake," Jessica warned. She twirled in front of the full-length mirror on the bathroom door, checking to make sure her sundress looked all right. Then she ran a comb through her long blond hair and was ready to go. As she walked out the door she said, "I'll see you later, Lizzie. If you happen to change your mind—"

"I won't," Elizabeth insisted. Sometimes Jessica didn't understand her at all, she thought.

As soon as Jessica was gone, Elizabeth began her work. But as she reread what she'd written, she decided that she didn't like it. She tore the sheet of paper from her typewriter, crumpled it into a ball, and tossed it in the trash basket. Using a fresh sheet, she started her story again. But she didn't like her second attempt any better. For some reason her ideas just weren't flowing. Maybe it was because the house was too quiet. She wasn't used to that. Normally Steven's stereo would be blasting and Jessica would be barging into her room every five minutes.

Elizabeth sighed and stared at yet another blank piece of paper in front of her. She was desperately trying to come up with an idea when she heard a knock at her door. "Honey, may I come in?" called Mrs. Wakefield.

"Sure, Mom," answered Elizabeth.

The door opened and Mrs. Wakefield walked in, her purse under her arm and sunglasses perched on her head. "I'm going to the mall, and I wondered if you'd like to take a ride with me," her mother asked.

It sounded like fun, and Elizabeth hesitated for a moment. "I don't think so. I'm trying to write a story, and I'm having trouble getting started," she explained.

"Then maybe you need to take a break. Sometimes it helps to clear your thoughts for a while," her mother suggested. "Also, I thought you might want to get a card for Mr. Garvin."

"Hey, that's a great idea!" Elizabeth exclaimed, her face lighting up. She had wanted to do something for her teacher, but until now she wasn't sure what. Deciding that a break might be just what she needed, Elizabeth jumped up and followed her mother outside to the car.

When Jessica arrived at the Fowlers' house a butler greeted her at the front door and escorted her out back. There, Jessica was dazzled by what she saw. Newly constructed bleachers framed the Fowlers' tennis court, a huge tent had been erected on the grounds, and people of all ages were milling about. And in the middle of the lawn, surrounded by adoring fans, cameras, and reporters, stood Chris Crosby. Jessica gasped. It was incredible seeing someone so famous in person.

Just then Lila came over to Jessica. "Ithig*so* *ni*thig*ice* ithig*to* sithig*ee* *y*ithig*ou*," she said with a broad smile as she linked arms with Jessica.

Jessica grinned back, happy that they were friends again. "Would you like something to eat?" Lila asked. "There are all sorts of things under the tent." She pointed to the long tables heaped with delicious-looking food. But before Jessica could answer, Ellen Riteman came running up to them, so excited she could barely speak.

"Look at this!" she said breathlessly, holding up a napkin that bore Chris Crosby's autograph. "I can't believe it!" she shrieked. "He actually signed my napkin!" Several of the other Unicorns, including Janet, Mary, and Betsy Gordon, gathered around to take a look. They were all very impressed. Celebrities were high on the Unicorns' list of important people.

Tapping Jessica on the shoulder, Julie Porter asked, "Where's Elizabeth?"

"Uh, she wasn't feeling well," Jessica fibbed, not knowing what else to say. She was sure Elizabeth wouldn't want her to tell everyone why she really stayed away.

"That's too bad," Julie said, her friendly brown eyes showing concern. "Tell her I hope she feels better."

"Sure," said Jessica with a grin. Then she spotted her brother coming in with his friend Ted Rogers. Having a bit of a crush on Ted, Jessica excused herself and walked over. "Hi, guys," she greeted them.

"Hi, Jessica," said Ted. "Where's your sister? I told her I'd give her some riding pointers soon." Ted worked after school at Carson Stables and was always helpful to Elizabeth, who loved horses.

"Uh, she's not feeling well," Jessica repeated.

"I'm sorry to hear that. Well, as soon as she gets better tell her to come down to the stables—"

"She's sick?" Steven interrupted. "When did that happen? She seemed fine when I saw her this morning."

Shooting him a mean look, Jessica discreetly nudged him with an elbow.

Mr. Fowler announced through a microphone that the match would be starting soon. The grown-ups were taking their seats in the bleachers. "We have our own special section," Lila informed her friends, pointing to the folding chairs that had been set up on the grass. The Unicorns and all the other kids from school rushed to get seats.

Jessica sat in one of the chairs next to Lila, and Amy sat in the other. Frowning at Jessica, Amy said to Lila, "What's she doing here?"

"I changed my mind and invited her," Lila said, brushing off the question. Then Lila turned to Jessica and said, "Ithig*I* githig*ot* ithig*to* mithig*eet* Chrithig*is* earlithigiithiger."

"Withig*ow*! Whithig*at* dithig*id* ithig*he* sithig*ay*?" Jessica asked.

"Ithig*he* sithig*aid*, 'Nithig*ice* ithig*to* mithig*eet* yithig*ou*,'" Lila said proudly.

"Withig*ow*!" Jessica repeated.

"By the way, where's Brett Carter?" Jessica whispered.

"Unfortunately, ithig*he* cithig*ould*ithig*n't* mithig*ake* ithig*it*," Lila said.

When Amy heard the two of them speaking Ithig, she became very upset. "Hey, when did you learn to speak that language, Lila?" she asked angrily, her voice rising. "Why didn't you tell me?"

"I was just about to," Lila informed her. "There's nothing to it. All you do is stick an 'ithig' in each syllable of a word. S*ithig*ee h*ithig*ow ithi-ge*a*s*ithig*y *ithig*it *ithig*is?" she told her.

"Is that all?" Amy asked, surprised. "*Thithi*-g*at* s*ithig*eems r*ithig*eal eas*ithig*y," she added, getting the hang of it.

After overhearing Lila, everyone around them picked it up. Soon they were all speaking Ithig. "*Thithig*is *ithig*is f*ithig*un!" Jessica heard Janet say.

"I*thig*it s*ithig*ure *ithig*is," Ellen answered.

Then the game started and they all quieted down. Chris Crosby's opponent was a local talent from the Sweet Valley Tennis Club. But he was no match for a professional like Crosby. Whenever he scored a point, everyone in their section would jump up and yell, "Y*ithig*ea, Cr*ithig*osb*ithig*y!"

By the end of the afternoon, after winning three out of five sets, Crosby won the match. The moment he scored the winning point, the crowd rose to their feet, breaking into cheers and applause. Crosby lifted his arms up in the air and took a bow while the spectators cheered him on.

Though not a big sports fan, Jessica thought this was one of the most thrilling moments of her life. Joining the others, she stood and clapped until her hands hurt.

When Jessica arrived home she ran straight upstairs to Elizabeth's room. "How did it go?" Elizabeth asked, looking up from her typewriter.

"Oh, Lizzie, it was fantastic! Chris Crosby is an unbelievable player. It was almost like being at Wimbledon! You really should've come. Have you been writing all day?"

"On and off. But I'm almost done." Elizabeth sighed. For once maybe Jessica was right. Perhaps she should have gone to the party. She could have put up with Lila for something so special. But it was too late to worry about it now, she thought.

Elizabeth turned around in her chair and forgot about her book for the moment. "Tell me everything," she urged her sister. "Wait a minute. Before you start, I want to show you something," Elizabeth interrupted herself. "I took a ride to the mall with Mom earlier and got this card for Mr. Garvin." She pulled out the card and showed it to Jessica.

Jessica cooed, pointing to the picture of the baby swaddled in a blue blanket. She opened it.

"'Congratulations from the two of us,'" she read aloud. "Oh, Lizzie, it's just perfect!"

Elizabeth handed her a pen, and Jessica quickly signed her name under her sister's. Then Elizabeth put the card in its envelope and looked at her attentively. "OK, continue," she said.

"Well, Crosby won, of course," Jessica began. But before she could go on, the phone rang. Jessica leaped up, ran into the hall, and picked up the receiver. "Hello?" she said.

"Is that you, Jessica?" a voice asked angrily.

"Amy?" Jessica guessed.

"Please put your sister on," Amy requested coldly.

Jessica called for Elizabeth. As she handed her the phone, she covered it and whispered, "It's Amy, and she sounds upset about something."

"Hello, Amy?" Elizabeth said into the receiver, unable to imagine why Amy was suddenly calling her. It had been nearly a week since they'd last spoken.

"Hello, Elizabeth. I just wanted to tell you that your dear sister told Lila about Ithig. What do you have to say about that? I mean, if Jessica told Lila, why couldn't you tell me? Apparently it wasn't such a big secret after all. . . ."

"Amy, we've got to talk. Listen, I'll be happy to tell you the secret whenever you like. It's really simple."

"It's too late," Amy interrupted. "I already know your dumb secret. And so does everybody else. Thanks, but no thanks," she yelled as she slammed down the phone.

What did Amy mean? Had Jessica told everyone? Elizabeth wondered. But more important, would Amy ever be her friend again?

On Tuesday afternoon Elizabeth walked into the music room for her weekly music class. She expected to find everyone sitting at their desks and Mr. Garvin at the front of the room. Instead she found a noisy group of kids. "Where's Mr. Garvin?" she asked as she walked over to her desk.

"Nobody knows," Sophia answered, shrugging her shoulders.

"Maybe he's sick," suggested Charlie Cashman, who also sat near Elizabeth. "Wouldn't it be great if class was cancelled?" he added hopefully.

"You want Mr. Garvin to be sick? That's terrible, Charlie," Elizabeth said, raising her voice over the noise in the room, which was getting louder and louder. Kids in the class were yelling, walking around, sitting on their desks, and in general taking advantage of the fact that no teacher was present.

Then a tall, young-looking woman entered the room. Everyone turned to look at her as they scrambled to their assigned seats. The woman went to the front of the room, stood behind Mr. Garvin's desk, and faced the students. "My name is Ms. McDonald," she announced, smiling nervously.

"As you all know by now, Mr. Garvin and his wife just had a baby. Mr. Garvin has since decided to take a leave of absence so he can help out at home. I'm pleased to announce that I'm going to be his substitute for the remainder of the year," she informed them.

Elizabeth was happy to hear that Mr. Garvin and his new family were doing well, but she was also saddened that he wouldn't be teaching any longer. She hoped that Ms. McDonald, with her wavy brown hair and pretty blue eyes, would be as nice as he was.

Elizabeth heard people groan and mutter,

"Oh, no!" She guessed that almost everyone would miss their old teacher as much as she would.

"Guess we don't have to worry about any tests today," Charlie joked loudly.

His best friend, Jim Sturbridge, called out, "Since it's your first day, we won't have any homework, right?"

Then Elizabeth saw a paper airplane glide right past her nose.

Picking up a ruler, Ms. McDonald rapped it against her desk, saying, "Boys and girls, please settle down." For a brief time the room became totally silent. Then Ms. McDonald started the lesson she'd planned. "Mr. Garvin was teaching you the history of different musical instruments, correct?" she began. No one answered her question, but she continued. "Today I'm going to play several different recordings and I want you to tell me which instruments you hear."

She walked over to the record player and put on an album. But as soon as she turned her back, the kids started talking and laughing.

"Hey, Charlie, catch this," Jim Sturbridge shouted, throwing the purse he'd just snatched off Lila's desk across the room.

"Jim! How dare you!" Lila cried. She rose from her seat and ran over to grab her purse from Charlie's hands. But by the time she got there, Charlie had already tossed it back to Jim. When Ms. McDonald turned around, Lila was standing in the middle of the center aisle.

"Just what do you think you're doing?" Ms. McDonald asked her.

"I'm trying to get my purse," Lila answered, pointing to the object that Jim was holding under his desk.

"Is that her purse?" the teacher asked Jim.

But Jim, a bully and a class clown, didn't say a word. Instead he pointed to his throat and silently mouthed, "I can't speak. I've got laryngitis." All the kids immediately burst out laughing.

Elizabeth saw Ms. McDonald's face turn red as she looked furiously at him. "Answer me!" she demanded, losing her patience. "If you don't give me an answer, I'll be forced to give you a week of detention," she threatened.

With this, Jim spoke up. "I'm sorry, Ms. McDonald, ithig*I* rithig*eall*ithig*y* ithig*and* trithigu-lithig*y* ithig*am*." He got up and gave Lila her purse.

"What?" the teacher asked, looking confused.

"Nithig*evithig*er *mithig*ind," Jim replied with a cunning smile.

Elizabeth was shocked that Jim Sturbridge knew Ithig. She remembered Amy saying that the secret was out and everybody knew it. At the time she thought Amy was exaggerating, but now she knew it was true. Most of the other kids were laughing hysterically at what was going on. Ms. McDonald's face was red and she looked as if she were about to start crying. She pounded her desk, trying once again to bring the class to order, but it was no use.

"*Hithig*ere, *cithig*atch *thithig*is," Charlie yelled to Jim as he tossed him an apple that he'd taken from his book bag. Then Jim threw the apple to Jerry McAllister, who started to eat it.

"*Cithig*an *ithig*I *hithig*ave *ithig*a *bithig*ite?" someone called from the back of the room.

"*Ithig*me *tithig*oo!" shouted someone else.

Elizabeth couldn't believe her classmates could be so cruel. After all, there didn't seem to be anything wrong with Ms. McDonald. The way the kids were acting was terribly unfair. No one even gave her a chance.

Ms. McDonald was so upset, she couldn't say a word. Everyone was speaking Ithig, and she couldn't understand a word they were saying. She sat at her desk with her head in her hands as the students continued to carry on. When she looked up, her eyes were red and her face was sad. Elizabeth desperately wanted to help her, but how?

Eight

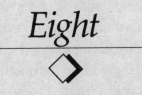

"Oh, I'm sorry, I was looking for Mr. Bowman. . . ." Amy apologized as she opened the door to his empty classroom and found Elizabeth sitting alone, working at one of the desks.

"He already left. He said something about a dentist's appointment," Elizabeth explained as she looked up.

"I had a question about our next assignment, but it can wait till tomorrow. . . . I didn't mean to disturb you." Amy started to close the door.

"No problem," Elizabeth called, trying to be friendly. "By the way, I just read your article, and I think it's terrific."

"Oh, thanks. Thanks a lot. I worked really hard on it," Amy said, her face beaming with pride.

"Well, you did a great job. Your descriptions were so clear, I almost felt like I was there myself," Elizabeth complimented her.

"That's a really nice thing for you to say," Amy volunteered, adding, "especially after some of the things I've said to you recently."

Then both girls opened their mouths at the same time. "I've been thinking—" Elizabeth started. "I wanted to tell you—" Amy began. Breaking into laughter, they smiled at each other for the first time in more than a week.

With her head down, Amy walked over to where Elizabeth was sitting. "Listen," she said softly, her blue eyes misting over. "I've acted really silly. I don't know why I got so upset. I wouldn't blame you if you never forgave me. Things just aren't the same without you, though."

Elizabeth was so happy, she felt like crying. Forgiving Amy at once, she said, "I've missed you, too, and I'm really sorry about—"

"Shh," Amy interrupted, holding her finger to her lips. "I'm the one who should apologize. I'm the one who acted like a spoiled brat. You didn't do anything wrong, Elizabeth. If you and Jessica have a secret, that's your business. Lila had

me convinced that there was something more behind it—"

"I'm willing to forget the whole thing if you
are. *Frithigiends*?" Elizabeth asked, grinning
warmly.

"*Frithigiends!*" Amy declared, throwing her
arms around her friend and hugging her.

"We should celebrate," Elizabeth suggested
brightly.

"How about getting sodas at the Dairi
Burger?" said Amy.

"Sounds good to me." Elizabeth gathered together the papers on her desk. This was one time
when the *Sixers* would just have to wait, she told
herself happily.

Leaving school, Amy and Elizabeth walked
outside and saw Lila, Charlie, and Jim on the
lawn. They were all excitedly discussing something. As Elizabeth and Amy walked over to them,
they heard them saying, "This'll really do her in!
She's going to learn her lesson the hard way!"

When Lila saw them she called out, "Amy,
Elizabeth, come over here! We want to tell you our
plan."

"What's going on?" Amy inquired.

"What are you talking about?" said Elizabeth, puzzled.

"We're talking about that awful Ms. McDonald," Lila said, and sneered. "We've got the perfect plan for ruining her future in Sweet Valley," she continued meanly.

"But how do you know she's so bad? Nobody even gave her a chance. Maybe she's really nice," protested Elizabeth. Even before hearing the plan, she knew she wasn't going to like it.

"What do you mean? You saw how she acted!" Charlie shot back.

"If she'd yelled at you, believe me, you'd hate her, too," Lila cried. "She's so nervous, she doesn't know what she's doing!"

"I think she was the one who didn't give *us* a chance," Charlie added.

"And do you know what I heard?" Lila said. "This afternoon when I was in the office, I heard the secretary say that the district supervisor is coming to our music class next week. Ms. McDonald is probably being reviewed for a permanent position here—"

"So this is the plan," Jim interrupted, looking at Elizabeth and Amy. "When the supervisor comes to our music class we'll only speak Ithig, got it? Ms. McDonald's gonna go crazy, and she'll probably get fired right then and there," he explained, smirking.

"That's a horrible idea!" Elizabeth exclaimed.

"You can count me out," said Amy.

"I think it's brilliant," Lila declared. "Are you saying that you're not going to help us?" she asked.

"That's right!" Elizabeth and Amy shouted in unison.

"There are always one or two party poopers in the group," Lila hissed back at them.

"It doesn't matter," Jim commented with a snort. "We can pull it off without them."

"Why don't you think about what you're doing? It's an awful thing to do!" Elizabeth pleaded. But her classmates didn't pay any attention. She and Amy turned away and left. But all the way down the block they could hear Lila shouting, "Party poopers! Party poopers!"

When Elizabeth got home from the Dairi Burger that afternoon, she ran upstairs, dropped her books on her desk, and immediately went back outside. She climbed into the huge pine tree in the backyard and sat on the lowest branch. This was her "thinking seat," the spot she came to whenever she needed to be by herself and do some serious thinking.

In her mind all Elizabeth could see was the frustrated expression on Ms. McDonald's sad face. To Elizabeth, the teacher seemed young and inexperienced, not mean and nasty. It was almost unbearable to think about what the class had planned for her. Nobody deserved to be treated that cruelly, Elizabeth thought.

Suddenly she had a terrific idea. If she told Ms. McDonald the secret of Ithig, Lila's plan wouldn't work. The more Elizabeth thought about it, the more excited she became. Of course, if Lila or the others found out, they'd be furious with her. But that was a chance she'd have to take. It was the only way to help Ms. McDonald.

"Hi, Jessica," Elizabeth called, jumping up and waving as she saw her sister approaching the back door.

"Hi, Lizzie. What's new?" Jessica called.

"Nothing," replied Elizabeth. Though this wasn't exactly the truth, she had no intention of telling Jessica her secret. If Jessica slipped and told Lila, the plan would be ruined. She couldn't risk telling a single person.

Nine

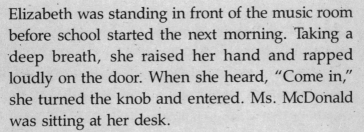

Elizabeth was standing in front of the music room before school started the next morning. Taking a deep breath, she raised her hand and rapped loudly on the door. When she heard, "Come in," she turned the knob and entered. Ms. McDonald was sitting at her desk.

"May I have a word with you, Ms. McDonald?" Elizabeth said softly.

"Yes, of course," the teacher replied.

"I'm Elizabeth Wakefield," Elizabeth said, walking across the room.

"I know," smiled Ms. McDonald, "and you have a twin sister named Jessica. Why don't you have a seat?" the teacher offered. Elizabeth liked her more already. She was really very friendly.

Elizabeth pulled up a chair and cleared her

throat. Trying to be delicate, she said, "You're probably aware that some of the kids, well . . . uh, they don't seem to get along with you. . . ."

That brought a smile to Ms. McDonald's face. "I would say that's putting it mildly," she admitted.

Elizabeth continued, "I hate to squeal, and it wasn't easy for me to do this, but the other kids are planning something really bad when the district supervisor comes. They hope you'll get fired. . . ."

Ms. McDonald remained calm. "What are they planning to do?" she asked.

Elizabeth kicked at the trash basket with the toe of her shoe. "Well, remember when they were speaking that strange language last week in class? It's called Ithig, and when the supervisor comes, that's *all* they're going to speak."

To Elizabeth's complete surprise, Ms. McDonald broke out laughing. "Ah, yes, the dreaded Ithig," she said, continuing to chuckle to herself.

"But I thought of a way to help you," Elizabeth explained. "If I told you how it works, you'd be able to understand what they were saying. Then you could explain to the district supervisor—"

Ms. McDonald interrupted with a question, "Yithig*ou w*ithig*ant* ithig*to t*ithig*each* ithig*me* Ithig?" She finished her sentence, folded her hands on her desk, and looked at Elizabeth.

Elizabeth couldn't believe her ears. *How did Ms. McDonald ever learn to speak Ithig?*

Sensing Elizabeth's surprise, the teacher explained, "I certainly hear it enough around this place. You kids seem to be obsessed with it. So I just figured out how it works by hearing it around school. It's really quite simple."

Elizabeth was very impressed that Ms. McDonald could pick up the language just by hearing it. Most people got so confused. . . .

Ms. McDonald laughed and said, "Elizabeth, how do you think children learn to speak? Or how do you think people learn foreign languages?" Ms. McDonald winked at her and added, "But I have a pretty good ear, if I do say so myself. After all, I'm a music teacher."

After a minute's thought Elizabeth realized that it made perfect sense—of course someone could figure out Ithig if that person had a good ear. Ms. McDonald was certainly proof of that.

"Now I feel silly," Elizabeth confessed.

"Whatever for?" the teacher asked.

"I had no idea you could speak Ithig," Elizabeth explained.

"Well, I couldn't a few days ago. But now I think I've got the hang of it," Ms. McDonald told her.

Then she rose to her feet and said, "Thank you for wanting to help me, Elizabeth. It's nice to have a friend."

"It only seemed fair," Elizabeth replied shyly as she got up to leave. She smiled to herself, thinking of the surprise that her classmates were going to have when they discovered that their secret language wasn't so secret after all!

Ten

◇

When Elizabeth's class filed into the music room the following week, the short, balding district supervisor had already arrived and was talking to Ms. McDonald.

Putting her hand to her head as if she had a headache, Amy groaned. "I'm not looking forward to this. Poor Ms. McDonald," she whispered in Elizabeth's ear as they took their seats.

Elizabeth nodded sympathetically. Meanwhile most of the other kids were giggling and looking at each other with mischievous glints in their eyes.

After everyone had taken a seat, Ms. McDonald stood up and said, "Hello, class. Say hello to Mr. Carruthers, the district supervisor. He'll be observing our class today." Already Elizabeth could hear the students snickering. But she was pleased to see that Ms. McDonald seemed much more relaxed and confident than she had during their first class.

"Hello, Mr. Carruthers," everyone said in unison, obeying their teacher like well-behaved students.

Ms. McDonald took attendance and then got down to business. "Now, did you all read the assignment?" she asked. Everyone nodded, indicating that they had. Elizabeth had never seen her classmates look so eager to get on with a lesson.

"The chapter described all the different types of string instruments. Are there any questions?" the teacher asked.

Immediately a sea of hands waved in front of her. But Lila Fowler raised her hand the highest and shook it the hardest. "Yes?" said Ms. McDonald, calling on Lila.

Lila cleared her throat, "I was wondering," she said, "Ithig*are* ithig*a* *p*ithig*ian*ithig*o* ithig*and* ithig*a* *h*ithig*arps*ithig*ichord* *t*ithig*he* *s*ithig*ame*?" By the time she got the whole sentence out, everyone was laughing hysterically.

But Ms. McDonald acted as if nothing was the slightest bit out of the ordinary. She patiently listened to Lila. Then she answered, "That's a very good question, Lila. *Tithighe* ithig*answ*ithig*er* ithig*is* ithig*no. Bithigut th*ithig*ey're b*ithig*oth str*ithig*ing* ithig*instr*ithig*umi*thig*ents*. Does that answer it for you?" she said matter-of-factly.

Lila was so shocked, her mouth hung open. Elizabeth smiled. Her classmates were all looking at one another with wide eyes. She overheard Lila hissing at Jim Sturbridge, "What happened?"

"Someone must have snitched, but it wasn't me," Jim shot back.

"I want to know who it was," Lila whispered, enraged. She looked around the class accusingly. But, of course, no one admitted to being the culprit. Sitting back in her chair, Elizabeth was pleased with the way things were going.

The teacher continued, "Sorry about this little interruption, Mr. Carruthers. We just had an exchange in a language called Ithig. It's a secret language the sixth graders have. I'd teach it to you, but it's their secret," she said, pointing to the students.

What a nice thing for her to do, thought Elizabeth. Even Charlie was surprised.

"Can you believe it?" he muttered under his breath. "She didn't even tell."

"I have some recordings that I want to play for you now," Ms. McDonald continued, going over to the record player. "Let's see how many different string instruments you can hear," she instructed, putting the needle on the record.

The orchestral sounds of a beautiful symphony filled the classroom. Soon, everyone was listening closely, interested in the lesson. And no one said another word about Ithig. Maybe Ms. McDonald wasn't such a bad teacher after all.

After class, while most of the kids rushed for the door, Amy stopped by Elizabeth's desk and sat on the edge as Elizabeth collected her things. "I guess Lila's plan was a real bomb!" Amy chuckled. "I thought I was going to die laughing when Ms. McDonald started speaking Ithig! Lila was so mad, I thought smoke was going to come out of her ears!"

"I know." Elizabeth laughed. "Lila looked as if she didn't know what hit her!"

"But isn't it strange that Ms. McDonald suddenly knew Ithig? I mean, she didn't know it last week. Somebody must have told her. Was it you?" Amy wondered out loud, tugging at her hair absentmindedly.

Elizabeth shoo̶ truthfully. "Maybe M̶ to figure it out for her̶

"Hey, want to con̶ afternoon?" Amy asked a̶

"Sure. I don't even̶ house looks like," Elizabet̶ hanging out at Amy's ever̶ ment over Ithig.

"Oh, Elizabeth," Ms. McD̶ ̶ ̶ ̶d called as the girls were walking into the hall. When Elizabeth turned around, the teacher was standing with Mr. Carruthers, a big, warm smile on her face. "Thank you again," she said, looking straight at Elizabeth. She winked. Elizabeth just smiled back at her as she left the room.

"Huh? What did she mean by that?" Amy asked suspiciously as soon as they were out in the hall.

Elizabeth just smiled mysteriously and pointed to the group of kids gathered in the corner. Lila was at the center of the group, making a big fuss about her foiled plan.

"When I find the squealer, there's going to be big trouble," Lila threatened, her pretty face twisted into an angry scowl.

on Lila," said Jim Sturbridge. "Just
The plan didn't work, that's all. You
have to get nasty about it."

Ellen Riteman agreed with him. "We'll probably never know who the backstabber was," she
said, shaking her head.

"I don't think she's so bad after all. It was
really neat that she kept our secret," Charlie
Cashman remarked.

"That's not the point," Lila hissed.

At that moment the door to the music room
opened and Mr. Carruthers came out. Recogniz-
ing the sixth grade students, he walked up to them
and said in a friendly voice, "How do you like
your new music teacher? I think she'll be a nice
addition to the school. What do you think?" he
asked earnestly.

Lila's face lit up in a cunning grin. Straighten-
ing her shoulders, she stood up tall. "If it were
up to me, I'd get someone else," she told the
supervisor.

He raised his eyebrows, looking concerned.
"Is there something I don't know about Ms. Mc-
Donald that I should?" he said, bending his head
attentively.

"Mr. Carruthers," said Lila, "I just don't like

her. Personally, I think she's a bore. Even the music she played was boring. . . ."

Elizabeth was furious at Lila for acting like a spoiled brat. She was so outraged that she was about to say something.

But Mr. Carruthers beat her to it. His friendly smile disappeared and he said in a sharp tone, "Young lady, I'm not interested in your musical preferences. Do you have any valid reasons for not liking Ms. McDonald?"

Lila seemed stunned by his change of manner, and just stood there stammering and clearing her throat.

"Does anyone else have anything they want to say?" Mr. Carruthers asked the group.

"I think she's very good," Amy immediately volunteered.

"Yeah, she's not so bad," Charlie admitted.

Lila whipped her head around and glared at them, horrified that no one was sticking up for her. Even Ellen, who usually agreed with everything Lila said, didn't come to her defense.

"If I were you, I'd spend more time with my books and less time causing trouble," the supervisor told Lila sternly. With that he turned on his heel and walked away.

Lila's face turned bright red. "No one talks to me that way," she sneered as soon as he was out of earshot.

"Let's get out of here," Jim said to Charlie, slapping him on the back. Then he called to Lila, "Next time you have a great plan, don't call me!"

The boys scooted around the corner and ran down the stairs, hooting and hollering at the top of their lungs. "Whithig*at* ithig*a* *d*ithig*umb* ithig*i*dithi-g*ea*!" shouted Jim.

"Lila," Ellen said softly, trying to put her hand on Lila's shoulder.

But Lila snapped nastily, "Leave me alone!" and ran down the hall.

On their way to Amy's house, Amy turned to Elizabeth and said, "You *did* teach Ms. McDonald Ithig, didn't you?"

Elizabeth looked her best friend directly in the eye. She wanted to be honest, but she also didn't feel that she had to defend herself. "No," Elizabeth replied. And that was the truth, because the teacher had figured it out on her own. But that was Ms. McDonald's secret.

"Then what was she thanking you for?" Amy asked suspiciously.

"For being a friend," Elizabeth answered simply.

They were walking past Mary Robinson's house when they heard someone shout. "Did you hear that?" Elizabeth gasped.

"It came from Mary's house," said Amy.

"I think we should check this out," Elizabeth said.

The two girls walked hesitantly up the path to the front porch. "Anybody home?" they called as they knocked on the door.

Just then the door flew open. Mary stood before them, her face red and tears streaming down her cheeks.

"Mary! What's wrong?" Elizabeth cried.

Mary took one look at their frightened faces, then burst into hysterical laughter.

"What's the matter with you?" Elizabeth cried, alarmed.

"It's not what you think. . . ." Mary stammered. "I just heard the most wonderful news. . . ."

Mrs. Robinson poked her head out of the kitchen and called out cheerfully, "Elizabeth, Amy, come in. We have some great news to tell you!" She came to the door and invited them into the sitting room.

Until recently Mary and her mother were separated for many years. Mary spent most of her life in foster homes, but she always believed that her real mother would return. And, miraculously, she did. Now they lived happily together in Sweet Valley.

"Tell them," Mary excitedly urged her mother as the girls took seats.

Mrs. Robinson sat on the arm of Mary's chair and started to giggle. "Well," she began, giving Mary's hand a squeeze. "Tim has asked me to marry him, and I've accepted. We're finally going to have a real family."

Amy and Elizabeth jumped out of their seats and ran over to hug Mrs. Robinson. "Congratulations! That's wonderful!" they screamed.

"And they're going to have a beautiful wedding and both of you are invited," Mary declared, her eyes gleaming.

"That's right. Elizabeth, I want your parents and your sister to come. Your family's been so kind and helpful to us ever since we moved here," said Mary's mother with a sweet smile.

"I'm sure they'll be honored," Elizabeth said warmly. She had a special feeling for Mrs. Robinson. With her blond hair and blue eyes, she reminded Elizabeth of her own mother. "Especially Jessica. She adores weddings," Elizabeth added.

"Will you do me a favor?" Mrs. Robinson asked her.

"Sure," Elizabeth replied eagerly. "What is it?"

"I was going to ask you to keep quiet about this just till we send out the invitations and make it official. It won't be long, because Tim and I want to get married as soon as possible," said Mrs. Robinson, then held her face in her hands and started giggling all over again.

The girls laughed at her, but in a good way. Her girlish joy made her seem more like a friend than one of their mothers.

Elizabeth was happy for both of them, but most of all for Mary. Her life had changed remarkably in the last few months. It wasn't long ago when Mary thought she might not have any family in the world.

"I won't say a word," Amy assured everyone. Then she added, "But it won't be easy, because this is incredible news!"

"And I'm good at keeping secrets," Elizabeth promised. It was lucky that Jessica wasn't there, Elizabeth thought with a grin. In a million years

Jessica wouldn't be able to keep quiet about a secret this big!

After walking home from Amy's later that day, Elizabeth burst through the door of the Wakefields' house. "Anybody home?" she called out.

Jessica came out of her room and called back from the head of the stairs, "Hi, Lizzie. Where have you been?"

As Elizabeth ran up the steps, she casually replied, "With Amy and Mary." Every time she thought about Mary's mother, she had to bite her lower lip to keep from grinning. She dropped her books and sat down on the top step next to Jessica. Though she was overflowing with excitement about the wedding, she didn't dare let on.

But Jessica wasn't fooled for a moment. She took one look at her sister's face and said, "Something happened. Tell me."

But Elizabeth just shrugged her shoulders as if she didn't know what her sister was talking about.

"Elizabeth Wakefield!" Jessica yelled, playfully pinching Elizabeth's arm. "I know you better than you think! You're keeping something from me, I know it."

"All right, I won't deny it. But it's a secret, and I can't tell you," Elizabeth confessed.

"A secret?" Jessica shrieked. "What do you mean you can't tell me? You can't tell your own flesh and blood? Your only twin in the world?" Jessica went on in dramatic outrage.

"You'll find out soon enough," Elizabeth said with a mischievous smile.

"Please, Lizzie," Jessica pleaded in her sweetest voice. "I promise I won't tell anyone."

Elizabeth broke out laughing. "With your track record? You expect me to believe that?" she kidded Jessica.

A week later Jessica and Elizabeth came home from school and found two ivory-colored envelopes, one addressed to each girl, waiting on the hall table.

"I wonder who they're from?" Jessica cried excitedly as she tore open her envelope.

"We'll soon find out," declared Elizabeth, opening hers at the same time. Though she knew exactly whom it was from, she didn't let on.

"Maybe these are the invitations to Mrs. Robinson's wedding," said Jessica. "Yes, I'm right! This is so exciting!" she exclaimed.

Elizabeth was shocked. "You knew about the wedding?" she asked.

"Oops," said Jessica. "I wasn't supposed to tell. You see, Mary swore me to secrecy. But I guess it doesn't matter now," she went on.

Just then the front door opened and Mr. Wakefield entered, carrying his briefcase. He'd just gotten home from work. "*Hithigow* ithig*are* ithig*my* fithig*avi*thig*ori*thig*ite twi*thig*ins*?" he asked with a smile.

"Guess what? Mrs. Robinson's getting married and we're all invited to the wedding," Jessica shouted. There was another invitation for Mr. and Mrs. Wakefield, which Jessica grabbed and showed to her father.

"*Thi*thig*is* ithig*is* g*ri*thig*eat*!" he exclaimed, looking it over. "*Withige'll hithigave* ithig*a bithig-gall*!"

"I can't wait. I just love weddings," said Jessica, holding the invitation to her chest.

"Why don't you two speak Ithig any more?" he wondered out loud as he took off his coat.

"It's not a secret, so it's not nearly as much fun," Jessica mused.

"Personally, I'm sick of secrets," admitted

Elizabeth. But at least Jessica was learning how to keep them, Elizabeth thought proudly.

"Besides, Dad, we've got much more important things to discuss than Ithig," Jessica announced.

"Oh, really? What's that?" asked Mr. Wakefield, looking slightly amused, but a little hurt.

"What we're wearing to the wedding, of course!" laughed Jessica.

Mr. Wakefield smiled understandingly. "Well, maybe you've lost interest in Ithig, *bithigut ithigI sithigure hithigavithigen't!*" he declared.

Is there yet another surprise in store for Mary's friends? Find out in **STRETCHING THE TRUTH,** *Sweet Valley Twins #13.*